GW01527302

Baby Sunflower enjoying the sun!

Smiling, laughing and having fun!

The bees are out...

...and the butterflies too!

The sun is bright…

...and the sky is blue!

The bees and the butterflies now have all gone...

Baby Sunflower lets out a yawn.

yawn

The sun is now setting to a beautiful tune...

Baby Sunflower has spotted the moon!

**The moon is now bright,
the day is now night.**

The sky is now sparkly and full of starlight!

**Yawn after yawn,
each one a surprise...**

Baby Sunflower closes it's eyes.

Goodnight Baby Sunflower!

The End.

Scan below for more Baby Sunflower!

Printed in Great Britain
by Amazon

20611630R00016